Erik and the Christmas Horse

by HANS PETERSON

Translated from the Swedish by Christine Hyatt

Illustrated by ILON WIKLAND

LOTHROP, LEE & SHEPARD CO. ❋ NEW YORK

First American edition 1970. Second printing June 1971. Copyright © Burke Publishing Company Limited 1969. Translated and adapted from the Swedish *Martin och farfars häst*.
First published in Sweden by Raben & Sjogren, Bokforlag, Stockholm, copyright © Hans Peterson and Ilon Wikland 1968. Library of Congress Catalog Card Number: 74-81926 Printed in Great Britain

Erik, who lived in the city of Göteborg in Sweden, had been waiting for a long time for the snow to come. He was lonely, for there were no other children in the building where he lived with his mother and father. In fact, there were no other children in the whole street. "If it snowed," thought Erik, "I could build a snowman—and maybe even an igloo."

On Wednesday Erik awoke very early. It was St. Lucy's Day, the thirteenth of December, and Christmas was not far off. It was so quiet that Erik wondered what was happening. He could not even hear the noise of traffic from the corner. All the usual sounds seemed muffled. He rushed to the window and looked out. At last it was snowing!

When Erik had finished his breakfast, he took his schoolbag and went downstairs, through the courtyard, and out into the street. The snow-covered ground was soft and white. The people in the street had snow on their clothes, but they all looked happy.

Suddenly Erik heard *clip-clop-clippity-clop*. He looked down the narrow street. There was old Mr. Lindberg with his cart-horse Mari coming to deliver packages.

Erik had known Mr. Lindberg and Mari for a long time. Today they looked especially sad. Mr. Lindberg's clothes were wet from the snow, and Mari's head drooped, almost touching the ground. As they clip-clopped into the courtyard, Erik rushed back to say hello.

"Oh dear," sighed Mr. Lindberg, "what Christmassy weather. You're lucky, Erik. You can run upstairs to your mother's kitchen and get warm. But it's not so good for many other people who have nowhere to live."

Erik had often wondered where Mr. Lindberg and his brown horse lived. Now he felt sure they must sleep somewhere under a bush at night or down by the water front. He thought of inviting them to come into his kitchen, but then he wondered how Mr. Lindberg could take Mari up the four flights of stairs.

At school that morning Erik thought only of Mr. Lindberg and Mari. His mind was not on the St. Lucy's Day celebration. He wished that Mari were a very little horse, just about the size of a dog, so that he could pick her up. Then he and Mr. Lindberg could take her upstairs to Mother's kitchen where it was nice and warm.

That afternoon, when Erik got home from school, Mr. Lindberg and Mari came back again. It was snowing even harder now and a cold wind was blowing. As Erik was patting Mari, Mr. Lindberg asked, "Why do you look so solemn, Erik?"

"I was wondering," said Erik, "if you and Mari could come to my house for Christmas."

Mr. Lindberg seemed surprised. He thought a minute, then said, "Yes, maybe we will visit you. But how would you like to take a drive with Mari and me right now?"

Erik thought that was a good idea.

"Then run upstairs and tell your mother," said old Mr. Lindberg.

Erik was soon sitting in the cart beside Mr. Lindberg, driving through the city. As Mari trotted along, snow drifted around her hooves. The streets looked beautiful as the snow swept along in white clouds. The Christmas decorations gleamed red, blue, and yellow. Down by the water front a tall Christmas tree swayed to and fro in the strong wind.

But all these lovely sights did not cheer Erik much.

As they drove over a bridge, Mr. Lindberg said, "Are you not enjoying the ride, Erik? What are you thinking about that makes you look so sad?"

"All the people who have nowhere to live—like you and Mari," said Erik quietly, still thinking how cold it must be for Mr. Lindberg and Mari under the bush at night.

Mr. Lindberg shook his head in amazement but he did not answer.

They passed a lot of traffic—cars and buses and motorcycles. And there was a long freight train going over the railway bridge.

Suddenly Mr. Lindberg seemed to have an idea. "It is getting colder," he said. "Wouldn't it be nice to have some tea and warm ourselves up a bit?"

"Then we must go home to Mother," said Erik quickly.

"That is a very kind offer, Erik," said Mr. Lindberg, "but we are already in Hisinger and I live not far from here. My wife is expecting Mari and me, and I'm sure she will enjoy having the company of a young friend."

Erik wondered if Mr. Lindberg's wife lived under the bush too, but he decided not to ask.

Mari clip-clopped quietly past the big shipyards. It was beginning to get dark. The snow was falling so heavily that Erik could hardly see the boats on the other side of the river.

"Perhaps Mrs. Lindberg could come home and have tea with us too," Erik said. "And we could put up a bed for her by the window. You could sleep on the kitchen sofa where I usually sleep and I could sleep on some cushions on the floor. And Mari could live down in the storeroom."

Mr. Lindberg heard all this but he did not answer.

"We will have such a happy time in the evenings," said Erik. "But you must come soon so that we can celebrate Christmas together."

Mr. Lindberg nodded thoughtfully but he still did not reply. Erik wondered what he was thinking about that made his face look so mysterious.

Now they were coming to a place with trees and beautiful wooden houses. Mr. Lindberg stopped Mari at the side of the road and gave her a bag full of oats. "Stay here," he said. "I'll be back soon."

As Mari ate her oats, Mr. Lindberg and Erik went into a yard to look at a stable. It was a little house which was very old.

"This is where Mari lives," said Mr. Lindberg.

"It is a very nice stable," said Erik.

Then they walked back to the street and Erik wondered why Mr. and Mrs. Lindberg did not live in Mari's stable too instead of out in the cold under a bush.

Mr. Lindberg took Erik by the hand and they trudged together up the steep hillside. It was quiet and peaceful here. There were little cottages with snow-covered gardens. The fruit trees and bushes were black and bare now because it was winter, but in summer they must be very pretty, Erik thought. A dog was barking and the snow was swirling in the wind. Down below lay the river and the water front. And on the other side of the river the lights of the city were glimmering.

Mr. Lindberg and Erik were standing in front of a little cottage. Mr. Lindberg opened the garden gate. As they went up the steps, the front door was opened by a woman.

"Welcome home," she said. "The tea is just made, and the cakes are fresh from the oven."

Mr. Lindberg smiled. "This is Mrs. Lindberg," he said to Erik, "and this is the house where we live." Then he turned to Mrs. Lindberg. "I have brought my friend Erik to tea."

They went inside the cottage and into the kitchen.
"Do you really live in this house?" asked Erik.
"Yes," said Mr. Lindberg, "this is our home."
"Then you don't live under a bush after all?"
"No," said Mr. Lindberg, smiling. "You are a fine
boy to say that we could come and live with you, but I
have brought you here to show you that we are lucky
to have a proper home of our own."

At first Erik felt very shy about having made such
a mistake. But then Mrs. Lindberg brought in her black
cat and that cheered him up.

After tea they set off in the cart again and soon Erik was back home.

It snowed all through that night, and it snowed for a whole week. Erik even built an igloo in the yard.

On the day before Christmas, Mari came clip-clopping down the street again. *Clip-clop-clippity-clop,* she went. In the cart sat Mr. Lindberg. He looked almost like a snowman.

"I am glad to see you," he said to Erik. "I have a parcel for you."

"For me?" said Erik in surprise. "May I open it now?"

"You must wait until this evening," said Mr. Lindberg. "I have brought you the parcel because you are such a fine boy."

In the evening Erik made a snow lantern out of snowballs. His mother lit a candle and Erik put it inside the lantern. The light shone out between the snowballs, over the yard and the igloo. Then Erik took out Mr. Lindberg's parcel and opened it carefully. Inside there was a brown wooden horse. It hung its head a little and it looked just like Mari. Erik put the wooden horse beside the snow lantern. It was just as though Mari had come clip-clopping out between great mountains of snow.

"Clip-clop-clippity-clop," whispered Erik softly as he patted the little wooden horse.

"Soon," he thought with a smile, "soon it will be Christmas."

F
P

Peterson, Hans

Erik and the
Christmas horse

DATE			
OCT 25		JAN 8	
DEC 15			
DEC 15			
SE 10 84		AP 17	
	JAN 07		

08917